Pocket Mommy

by Aila Malik & Zayan Verma

illustrated by Vincenzo Lara

Dearest Sofia —
~Your Godmom
always keeps you in
her heart!

Published by Mind's Eye Publishers

Copyright © 2013 Aila Malik

ISBN: 0615848206

ISBN 13: 9780615848204

Library of Congress Control Number: 2013901057

Createspace Independent Publishing Platform

North Charleston, South Carolina

Zayan was ready to start school. Tomorrow was going to be his first day!

As Mommy tucked Zayan into bed that night, Zayan said, "Mommy, I wish you could be with me the whole day. I miss you when I am not with you."

"Zayan, I love and miss you too. We are always together because we are inside of each other's hearts," said Mommy.

Suddenly, Mommy had an idea!

At night, when Zayan was asleep, she used cardboard, scissors, and colored pencils to make a little paper doll. It was a cardboard "mommy," just small enough to fit into Zayan's pocket.

The next morning, it was time for Zayan to go to school. He was feeling a little nervous again, but Mommy told him to *focus on one thing at a time.*

Zayan focused on brushing his teeth and washing-up, but tears kept rolling down his face.

Zayan focused on changing his clothes, but he couldn't seem to get all the buttons on his shirt to button up the right way.

Zayan focused on eating his breakfast, but he wasn't that hungry.

Then it was time to leave the house and get into his booster seat in the car.

On the way to school, Mommy told Zayan how proud of him she was for trying to focus on one thing at a time. She reminded him that she loved him and that they were in each other's hearts.

Just before they entered the school parking lot, Mommy pulled the car over into a tiny street alley.

Mommy turned around and gave Zayan a small envelope. She told him to open it carefully. Zayan opened the envelope, pulled out the small cardboard Mommy, and gave Mommy a big smile.

"That is Pocket Mommy. She will go with you to school, and you can take her out anytime you are feeling sad or nervous. When I pick you up, I want to know everything that Pocket Mommy did with you."

Zayan was so excited to get to school and put Pocket Mommy into the pocket of his jeans.

When they arrived at school, Mommy knelt down to hug Zayan. He hugged her back very tightly. Then after a few seconds, Zayan took a deep breath and let go of her neck. He quickly reached for his Pocket Mommy and waved goodbye to his real Mommy.

At school, Zayan sat in a circle while the teacher, Ms. Jessica, taught the class fun songs. He learned about the days of the week and talked about his favorite topic—animals at the zoo.

Then Zayan practiced writing letters and numbers with fun-colored pencils. He and his table friend shared all the pencils, even their favorite colors.

After writing time, Zayan played with musical instruments and listened to Ms. Linda, play the guitar. Everyone in the class took turns to strum the guitar and beat on Ms. Linda's drum.

Zayan was pretty hungry at lunchtime, but was also starting to miss his mommy. He took Pocket Mommy out of his pocket and put her on the table next to his lunch box. Daddy had packed him a yummy lunch—a peanut-butter and jelly sandwich, applesauce, string cheese, and a juice box. Zayan noticed that Tanner, one of his table friends, had the same juice box! Pocket Mommy seemed to smile at Tanner and Zayan as they poked their straws into their juice boxes.

After lunchtime, it was rest time. Zayan got to sleep on a mat next to Matthew, one of his classmates. He slipped Pocket Mommy under his pillow and closed his eyes, just for a minute. When he opened them, it was almost time for his real mommy to pick him up from school!

Just when Zayan started missing his mommy again, it was time to go play outside. There were so many fun things to play with, like balls and chalk.

There was even a giant play structure with a big slide!

Zayan pretended that the play structure was a ship, and he found a friend, Lucy, to play pirates with him.

Before he knew it, Zayan's mommy was calling his name. It was time to go home.

Zayan grabbed his lunch box and jacket and ran towards his mommy. He gave her a big hug. He was happy to see her.

That night, Zayan told his real mommy about his day and all the times that Pocket Mommy came out of his pocket and spent time with him.

Mommy told Zayan that she kept a picture of him in her purse. She told him that even though he was always in her heart, it helped her to know that she could see his face when she missed him the most.

"Zayan," Mommy said, "I am proud of you for going to your first day of school and for focusing on one thing at a time. You will see that tomorrow will be a little easier."

Mommy put Pocket Mommy on the nightstand and kissed Zayan goodnight.

The next day at school, Zayan knew what was going to happen. He ate lunch with Tanner, Lucy, and his new friend Jeff. During recess, he played soccer with six friends!

That week, Zayan took Pocket Mommy to school with him each day. When he felt nervous or started to miss his real mommy, he put his hand in his pocket and squeezed Pocket Mommy to give her a little hug. Every night he and Mommy talked about Pocket Mommy's adventures.

The next week, Zayan started to make a lot of friends. He knew everyone's name and really started having fun doing art, music, and other activities at school. Most days, Zayan was so busy with his friends that he forgot to put his hand in his pocket at all!

On the eleventh day of school, Zayan was getting dressed in the morning and was about to put Pocket Mommy in his pocket when he decided to make a different choice.

"Mommy," Zayan said.

"Yes, Zayan?"

"I think I should leave Pocket Mommy here in my room, because she is getting really torn in my pocket. Besides, I don't think I need her anymore. Do you know why?"

"Why?"

"Because we are always in each other's hearts forever!"

Mommy smiled and hugged Zayan tightly.

Instructions for Creating Your Own Pocket Person:

Simply cut out one of the Pocket People from the back cover of this book! You can glue your own picture on top of its face to customize the Pocket Person. Check our website to purchase a doll-like version of your Pocket Person: www.pocketmommy.org.

Pocket Mommy Debrief Conversation Ideas:

1. What did Pocket Mommy do or see today?
   - Use this question to learn how the day went for your children. What do your children remember from the day? Use this to gauge the overall tenor of the day.

2. When did you take her out of your pocket? What was happening at school?
   - This question can be a baseline as you progress through the week. If Pocket Mommy came out three times at the beginning of the week and then only one time later in the week, it is likely that the children are starting to feel more comfortable in school.
   - Note what was happening when Pocket Mommy came out and find patterns. You might learn that Pocket Mommy emerges during periods of transition or nap time (where there is a lack of structure or distraction) or even during a particular activity. You can use that information to help alert teachers to your children's periods of insecurity.

3. Did Pocket Mommy meet any of your new friends? Or your teacher?
   - This might tell you who your children are interacting with and who your children are comfortable expressing more of themselves with. The answer might also show that the children want to keep this coping tool (or maybe even the insecurity) as a secret.

4. What do you want to show Pocket Mommy tomorrow?
   - This prompt is designed to gently let the children know that they are going to school again tomorrow and to help build excitement for what the day might bring. It also helps remind the children that they know what to expect during the next school day.

Note from the Author:

I am an attorney and a nonprofit executive. I have dedicated my professional life to working with high-risk youth, using the law and human empathy as vehicles to build necessary life skills and teaching others to do the same. My most important job, however, is my family role as a wife and mother of three young children (ages seven, four, and two).

When my oldest child, Zayan, first went to preschool, he was, as most kids are, nervous about leaving home and being away from me for so many hours. I hit on an idea I called Pocket Mommy. I cut out a simple cardboard doll and drew my face on it and told Zayan that anytime he missed me, he could put his hand in his pocket and remember that I was thinking about him and missing him, too. I also told him he could take his Pocket Mommy out of his pocket and show her what was going on and tell her what he wanted to do next.

The idea worked beautifully. As you learn in the story, Zayan made very good use of his Pocket Mommy to make a successful transition to preschool and build new friendships. That was what I was hoping for and expecting.

What I didn't expect, however, was how Pocket Mommy triggered rich conversations at home. At the end of each day, I asked Zayan about when he had called on her. What he told me went far beyond typical conversations with a preschooler, and it was so revealing about how he was doing and how his day went.

The day that he told me that he was going to leave his Pocket Mommy at home gave me confidence that he had successfully transitioned into preschool and that I didn't need to worry about his anxiety anymore.

Ironically, that was exactly when I realized just how nervous my husband and I, as parents, had been about this transition. Knowing that Zayan had his Pocket Mommy with him calmed me as well, because I knew we had given him a tool to cope with his nervous feelings.

It is my hope that Pocket Mommy will be a helpful tool for you and your children during the critical home-to-school transition and give you new memories to share for years to come.

Sincerely,
Aila Malik

Meet the Pocket Mommy Team:

Pocket Mommy is Aila's first children's book. As a working professional and mom of three young children, Aila and her family created an innovative tool to help her young pre-schooler successfully master the home to school transition. Years later, Aila and her son share their story and tools in the hopes of making a difference with families in the same situation.

Aila has a Juris Doctorate from Santa Clara University and is a member of the California Bar. She has dedicated her professional life to working with high-risk youth—using the law and human empathy as a vehicle to build necessary life skills—and teaching others to do the same. Her most important job, however, is raising her little ones to "leave the world better than it was when they arrived!"

Aila co-authored *Pocket Mommy* with her now 7-year old, Zayan Malik Verma. Zayan recently finished first grade and is an avid fisherman, pianist, and athlete. Now that "being an author" is checked off his list, Zayan hopes to become a police officer or a scientist when he grows up.

Vincenzo Lara, long-time friend of the authors, illustrated *Pocket Mommy* with an edge that matched our Team's playful and unique personalities. His formal education is in graphic design but took up a love for drawing and illustrating around the age of 9 when his best friend, Oscar would draw exact replicas of baseball cards (mainly SF Giants players, obviously), prompting Vincenzo to find his own spark for art. Influenced by his interest in street art, better known as graffiti, Vincenzo furthered his artistic eduction at Academy of Art, San Francisco.

CPSIA information can be obtained at www.ICGtesting.com
Printed in the USA
LVIW01n1946260517
535941LV00002B/5